MATH MAN

MATH MAN

by **Teri Daniels**   illustrated by **Timothy Bush**

Orchard Books • New York

An Imprint of Scholastic Inc.

Library of Congress Cataloging-in-Publication Data
Daniels, Teri.
Math man / by Teri Daniels ; illustrated by Timothy Bush.
p.   cm.
Summary: In the fall, Mrs. Gourd and her class take a field trip to
the Mighty Mart, where they see plenty of math in action.
ISBN 0-439-29308-1
[1. Mathematics—Fiction. 2. School field trips—Fiction. 3.
Supermarkets—Fiction.] I. Bush, Timothy, ill. II. Title.
PZ7.D21955   Mat 2001   [Fic]—dc21   00-66585

10 9 8 7 6 5 4 3 2 1   01 02 03 04 05
Printed in Mexico   49

First edition, October 2001

The text of this book is set in 14 point Bookman.
The illustrations are watercolor.
Book design by Zara Design

Of all the food stores in town, the Mighty Mart was the most plentiful.

Mrs. Gourd led her class to the superstore
tour. "It's a fine way to see math in action," she said.
Marnie didn't give a bat's brain about math in action. It was
nearly Halloween, and all she could think of was buying a pumpkin,
big and bumpy.

Marnie jingled the loose change waiting in her pocket. She
liked the way it sounded.

The Mighty Mart was dressed for fall. Spiders clung to the candy shelves. Skeletons hung from the fruit bins. And scarecrows slumped over baskets brimming with dried corn.

Mr. Budget, the manager, zoomed past the ghost balloons bobbing at the entrance. He asked everyone nearby to sing the Mighty Mart promise: "We're the superstore with so much *more*!"

Garth, the stock boy, sang the loudest.

Marnie thought the song was dumb. "When do we get to buy pumpkins?" she asked.

"Best for last," said Mr. Budget, setting his sights on Garth. "Don't forget to fill the pumpkin bin," he warned.

Garth popped out his chest. "You can count on me, Mr. B."

Seconds later, a voice blared from above:

"EGG BREAKAGE IN AISLE EIGHT. . . . OIL SPILL IN NINE."

"How dreadful," said Mr. Budget, scurrying to check the mess.

"Wait!" cried Mrs. Gourd. "We were hoping to see math in action."

"Stick with me," said Garth. "My friends don't call me Math Man for nothing."

Garth loaded his price gun and repeated the Mighty Mart promise: "We're the superstore with so much *more!*"

Keep your eyes open! Math is everywhere!

Fun!

The class liked the way it sounded, especially the word *more.*

Even Marnie perked up. "Can I buy *more* than one pumpkin?"

"Sorry," said Mrs. Gourd. "One per customer."

"Watch this," said Garth.
Zap-zap-zap. He tagged bags
with a flick of his wrist.
Mrs. Gourd timed him. "That's
one hundred and twenty
bags per minute."
"Two bags per second,"
said Garth.

Okay, how
is that
expressed as
a math
equation?

120 bags ÷
60 seconds
= 2 bags
per second

Fun!

"Make way for sprouts," he shouted.
"Ten, twenty, thirty, forty . . ."
Mrs. Gourd's eyes shined like dimes.
"Splendid," she said. "Counting by
tens."

"I'm handy at hurling lettuce," said Garth. "Two, four, six, eight . . . Two heads are better than one."

Lettuce $1.29

"And I'm really super when I stack the spuds. One potato, two potatoes, three potatoes, four. Five potatoes, six potatoes, seven potatoes, *more!*"

Passing shoppers sang along. They liked the way it sounded, especially the word *more.*

Marnie hated potatoes. She wanted to buy a pumpkin.

Mrs. Gourd raved. "This place is a math bonanza!"

"You're one hundred percent right," said Garth, marching toward the melons. "We have all sorts of problems at the Mighty Mart."

"Try the quarter slices, Mr. Pit," Garth offered. "A whole watermelon is hard to fit in the fridge."

The children jumped in place, chanting, "*Four* quarters equal a *whole*."

"Exactly!" said Mrs. Gourd.

"I see trouble," said Garth, racing to the snack cakes. "There are *four* Dinkies in that box, ma'am. And you've got *five* kids. How about a family pack of *ten* . . . two snacks each?"

Ten Dinkies divided by five kids equals two Dinkies for each kid.

$10 \div 5 = 2$

—Fun!

"Aren't you the smart one," said the mom.

"Bat brains!" said Marnie. "I'm smart too." She counted her money out loud. "I have two quarters, four dimes, and ten brown pennies. That's a dollar for a pumpkin, big and bumpy."

$.25 + $.25 + $.10
+$.10 + $.10 + $.10
+$.01 + $.01 + $.01
+$.01 + $.01 + $.01
+$.01 + $.01 + $.01
+$.01 = $1.00

"A small, *one*-pound pumpkin costs only forty cents," said Garth. "A quarter, a dime, and five pennies." He sorted the coins on her palm. "The rest could be yours to keep."

Marnie's eyes widened as she figured out her change.

$1.00 − $.40 = $.60

Fun!

"How much is a bigger pumpkin?" asked Mrs. Gourd.

"A two-pound pumpkin costs eighty cents," Garth continued.

"Three pounds cost $1.20.
Four pounds: $1.60.
Five pounds: $2.00.
Six pounds: $2.40."
Faster and faster he multiplied in his head.
"Seven: $2.80.
Eight: $3.20.
Nine: $3.60.
And a *ten*-pound biggie costs a whopping $4.00!"

Garth had a way with numbers.

$$2 \times \$.40 = \$.80$$
$$3 \times \$.40 = \$1.20$$
$$4 \times \$.40 = \$1.60$$
$$5 \times \$.40 = \$2.00$$
$$6 \times \$.40 = \$2.40$$
$$7 \times \$.40 = \$2.80$$
$$8 \times \$.40 = \$3.20$$
$$9 \times \$.40 = \$3.60$$
$$10 \times \$.40 = \$4.00$$

whew!

Wow!

Fun!

It wasn't long before Garth's way with numbers got around. One shopper spread the word to two shoppers . . .

and they told two shoppers . . .

and they told two shoppers . . .

and they told two shoppers . . .

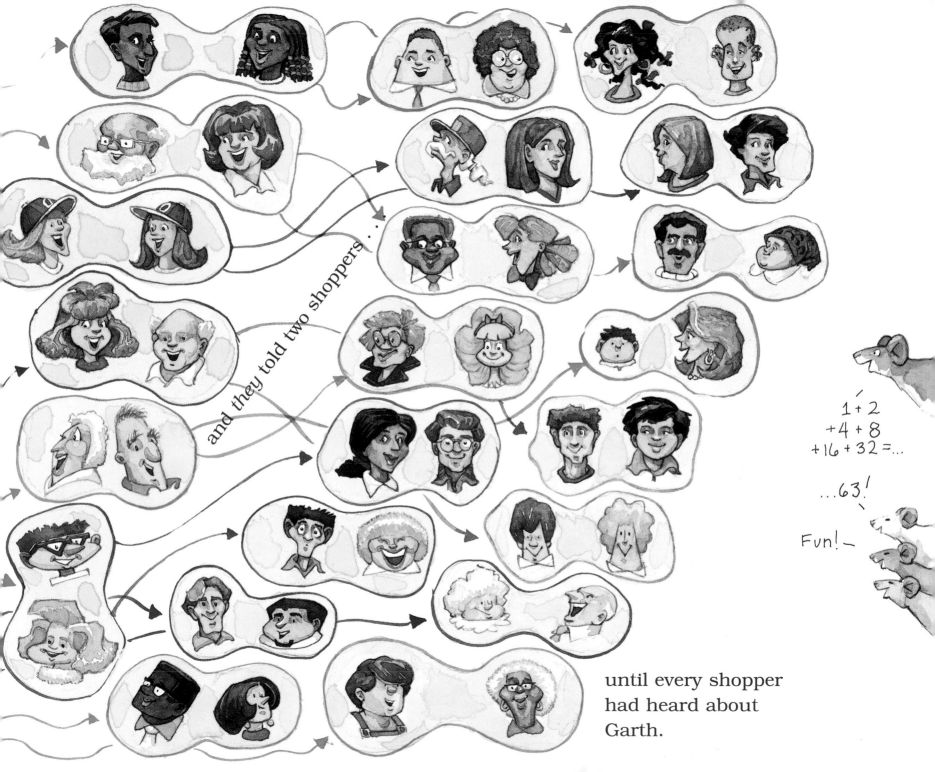

and they told two shoppers . . .

$1 + 2$
$+ 4 + 8$
$+ 16 + 32 = ...$

$...63!$

Fun! —

until every shopper
had heard about
Garth.

"Tour time!" cried Mr. Budget. He blew in like October wind and swept the class to the service desk. "My handy-dandy microphone can blast an urgent message:

Mighty Mart Feeeever!

COCO LOCO ICE CREAM
IS FIFTY PERCENT OFF!"

50% of $4.00 is...

$4.00

Coco Loco

$2.00

Mr. Budget rushed to the checkout to show off his scanners. "These nifty gadgets read each price with a thin laser light. We couldn't add the orders up without them."

Ping, ping . . . ping, ping, ping. "That's seven dollars and thirty-three cents," said the cashier. "Couldn't add the orders up without 'em."

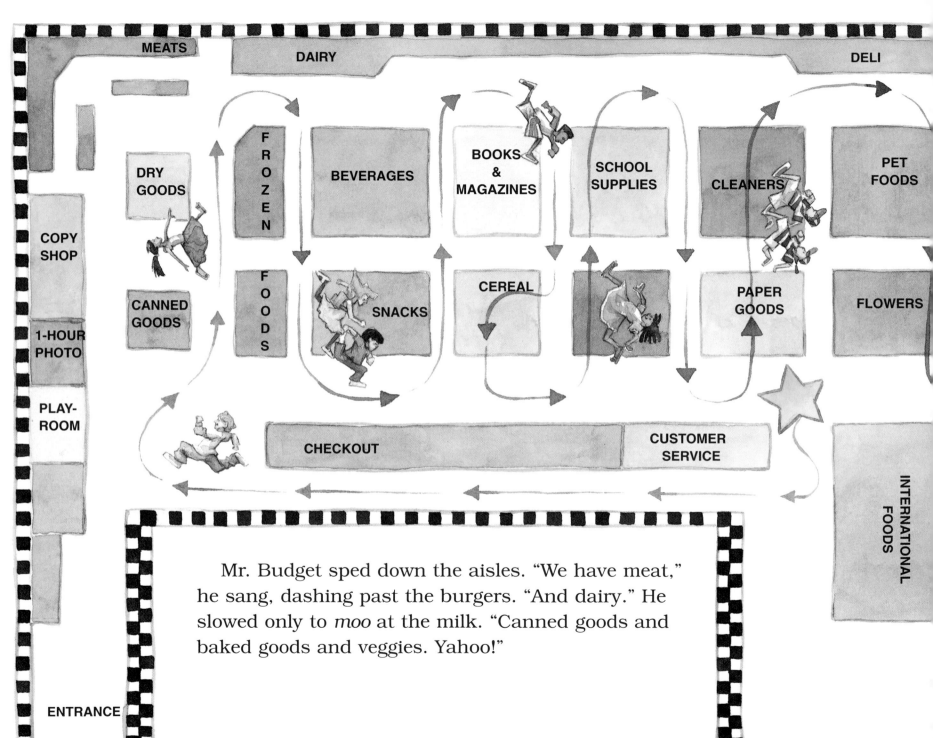

MEATS
DAIRY
DELI
PET FOODS
FLOWERS
INTERNATIONAL FOODS
CLEANERS
SCHOOL SUPPLIES
BOOKS & MAGAZINES
PAPER GOODS
BEVERAGES
CEREAL
SNACKS
FROZEN FOODS
DRY GOODS
CANNED GOODS
COPY SHOP
1-HOUR PHOTO
PLAY-ROOM
CHECKOUT
CUSTOMER SERVICE
ENTRANCE

Mr. Budget sped down the aisles. "We have meat," he sang, dashing past the burgers. "And dairy." He slowed only to *moo* at the milk. "Canned goods and baked goods and veggies. Yahoo!"

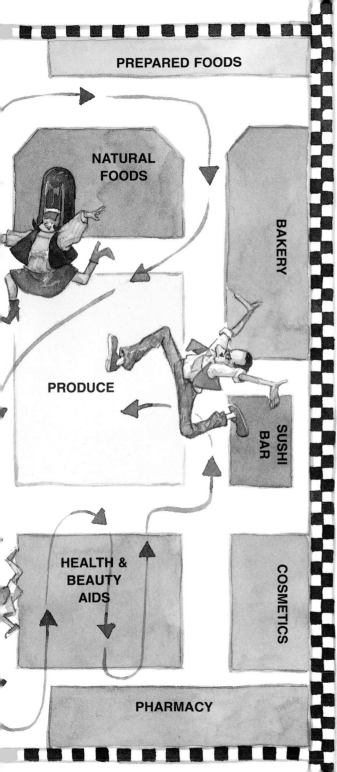

When they reached the Best Bet pumpkin bin, the tour came to a stop.

"Can we pick our pumpkins now?" Marnie asked.

Mr. Budget peered into the bin. He pulled out a single stump.

"Witch warts!" cried Marnie. "The pumpkin bin is empty!"

Mr. Budget glared at Garth. "Someone has forgotten the Mighty Mart promise."

Garth scrambled past the eggbeaters. "Have no fear," he shouted. "I'll fill that bin in a flash."

While Garth searched the stockroom, the Mighty Mart got
hit with the hardest problem of all.

Pow! **Ping!** **Zing!**

Bzzz . . . zz . . . *zonk.*

The superstore scanners went *kaput* . . .

That was close!

. . . and the puzzled cashiers couldn't add the orders up without them.

The Mighty Mart workers fiddled with the machines. Not one could fix them. They tried adding in their heads. That only made matters worse:

Let me see...
$1.50 + $3.50 + $1.30 ...

"Your total is six hundred and thirty dollars," said a cashier.

"For three items?" asked the shopper. "How can that be?" Sadly, no one knew.

The cranky customers gathered at the checkout, while Mrs. Gourd's class waited, hoping to pick out some pumpkins.

What was her mistake?

— She forgot the decimal point!

When Coco Loco ice cream leaked from sixty baskets on six long lines, Mr. Budget freaked.

"CAN'T ANYONE AROUND HERE ADD!!??"

$.25 + $.10 + $.01 + $.01 + $.01 + $.01 + $.01 = ...$.40.

—Fun!

Marnie raised a handful of money—a quarter, a dime, and five brown pennies. "It costs forty cents to buy a one-pound pumpkin," she said. "*Garth* told me."

Suddenly every shopper buzzed about Garth.

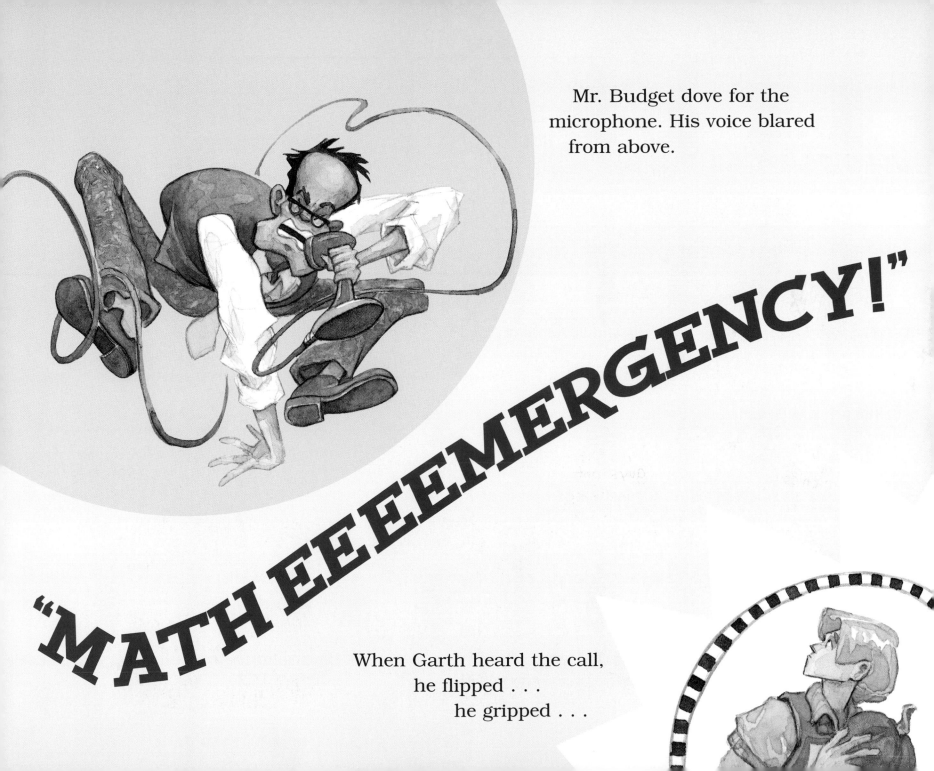

Mr. Budget dove for the microphone. His voice blared from above.

"MATH EEEEMERGENCY!"

When Garth heard the call,
he flipped . . .
he gripped . . .

. . . he *flew* into action.

"*Math Man to the rescue!*" he thundered. "Able to add sixty baskets with a single brain!"

Math Man added:

.69 +
$1.19 +
$2.49 +
$3.09 +
.99 +
$5.00 +
$2.29

...equals
$15.74

. . . until every order had been tallied.

"Our hero!" cried the children, crowding around the pumpkins. "This is the store with so much more."

Math Man laughed the loudest. "Pumpkins are our specialty."

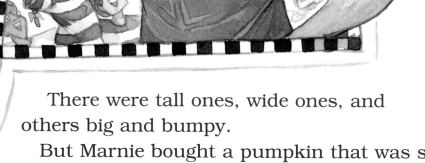

There were tall ones, wide ones, and others big and bumpy.

But Marnie bought a pumpkin that was small and smooth.

"One pound," said Garth, lifting it off the scale.

"I was hoping it would be," said Marnie. "Here's forty cents." She dropped seven coins on the counter and nine more in her pocket.

Marnie jingled the leftover change. She liked the way it sounded.

When all of the pumpkins were weighed and paid for, Garth grabbed a price gun and repeated the Mighty Mart promise. So did his willing assistant.

"Ready for action?" asked Garth.

Marnie giggled. "You can count on me."

Flap. Flap. Zap. Zap. They bagged and tagged ten candy-apple treats.

"One per customer," said Marnie.

Ten treats for nine kids plus one teacher equals...